# Chinchillas

Grace Houser

New York

Published in 2018 by The Rosen Publishing Group, Inc.
29 East 21st Street, New York, NY 10010

First Edition

Editor: Melissa Raé Shofner
Book Design: Mickey Harmon
Interior Layout: Rachel Rising

Photo Credits: Cover MirasWonderland/Shutterstock.com; Cover NatalT/Shutterstock.com; p. 5 VKarlov/Shutterstock.com; p. 7 zakharov aleksey/Shutterstock.com; p. 9 Kuznetsov Alexey/Shutterstock.com; p. 11 Roksolana Baran/Shutterstock.com; p. 12 AleksandrN/Shutterstock.com; p. 13 © iStockphoto.com/PhotoTalk; p. 14 279photo Studio/Shutterstock.com; p. 15 icealien/Shutterstock.com; pp. 17, 20 yevgeniy11/Shutterstock.com; p. 19 Patcharin Chatchirdchaikul/EyeEm/Getty Images; p. 21 OlgaBungova/Shutterstock.com; p. 22 Auscape/Universal Images Group/Getty Images.

Cataloging-In-Publication Data
Names: Houser, Grace.
Title: Chinchillas / Grace Houser.
Description: New York : PowerKids Press, 2018. | Series: Our weird pets | Includes index.
Identifiers: ISBN 9781508154235 (pbk.) | ISBN 9781508154174 (library bound) | ISBN 9781508154051 (6 pack)
Subjects: LCSH: Chinchillas as pets–Juvenile literature.
Classification: LCC SF459.C48 H68 2018 | DDC 636.935'93–dc23

Manufactured in the United States of America

CPSIA Compliance Information: Batch #BS17PK: For Further Information contact Rosen Publishing, New York, New York at 1-800-237-9932

# Contents

What Is It? . . . . . . . . . . . . . . . . . . . . . . . . .4

Big Ears, Soft Fur . . . . . . . . . . . . . . . . . . . . .6

Life in the Wild . . . . . . . . . . . . . . . . . . . . . .8

Your New Pet . . . . . . . . . . . . . . . . . . . . . . .10

A Place to Live . . . . . . . . . . . . . . . . . . . . . .12

What's for Lunch? . . . . . . . . . . . . . . . . . . . .14

Happy and Healthy . . . . . . . . . . . . . . . . . . . .16

Keeping Clean . . . . . . . . . . . . . . . . . . . . . . .18

Playing with Your Pet . . . . . . . . . . . . . . . . . .20

Chinchilla Care Fact Sheet . . . . . . . . . . . . . . .22

Glossary . . . . . . . . . . . . . . . . . . . . . . . . . .23

Index . . . . . . . . . . . . . . . . . . . . . . . . . . . .24

Websites . . . . . . . . . . . . . . . . . . . . . . . . . .24

# What Is It?

Is it a mouse? Is it a squirrel? Is it a rabbit? No, it's a chinchilla! If you've never seen one of these cute little creatures before, you might not be sure what it is at first. Once you pet one, though, you'll never forget. Chinchillas have really soft fur!

Chinchillas make great pets, but there are a few things you should know before bringing one home. Read on to find out if a chinchilla might be the pet for you!

PET FOOD FOR THOUGHT

Chinchillas can live for a long time—up to 20 years! Keep this in mind when considering one as a pet.

If you give your pet chinchilla lots of love and attention, it'll be your friend for a long time.

5

# Big Ears, Soft Fur

One of the first things you'll notice about chinchillas is that they have big, round ears. In the wild, their ears help them stay cool and listen for danger. Adult chinchillas are usually 9 to 15 inches (22.9 to 38.1 cm) long and can weigh up to 1.8 pounds (0.8 kg). They also have a long tail that helps them balance.

Chinchilla fur is very thick and soft. Their fur may be gray, white, black, tan, silver, or even a bluish color.

## PET FOOD FOR THOUGHT

If you're **allergic** to cats and dogs, a chinchilla may be a good pet for you. Chinchillas don't bother some people's allergies.

A chinchilla's fur is so thick that it protects the animal from **fleas**. However, fleas may still bite a chinchilla on its face, ears, and legs.

# Life in the Wild

There are two species, or kinds, of chinchillas: long-tailed and short-tailed. In the wild, chinchillas live high up in the Andes Mountains in South America. It can be quite cold there, but their thick fur keeps them warm. Hot weather is bad for chinchillas. They can overheat!

Chinchillas live together in large groups called herds. They like to hide in spaces between rocks or dig tunnels underground. Chinchillas are nocturnal, which means they sleep during the day. They're most active at sunrise and sunset.

PET FOOD FOR THOUGHT

If a chinchilla is caught by a predator, it will release a bit of its fur to escape. This is called a "fur slip." After a while, the fur will grow back.

By the early 1900s, chinchillas had been nearly hunted to **extinction** because so many people wanted their soft fur. It's now illegal to hunt wild chinchillas in several South American countries.

Chinchillas are small animals, but they still need lots of care. Make sure you have the time to care for one. If you decide to get a pet chinchilla, you can adopt one from an **animal shelter** or buy one from a pet store.

Chinchillas have lots of **energy** and can sometimes be a little nervous. They're not good pets for very young children. An energetic child might frighten or mistakenly hurt a pet chinchilla, which may cause the animal to bite.

**PET FOOD FOR THOUGHT**

It's believed that chinchillas are smarter than rabbits!

Do you want an adult chinchilla or one that's still young? A baby chinchilla is called a kit!

# A Place to Live

Chinchillas need a lot of room to run and jump. A large wire cage is the perfect home. However, the cage floor shouldn't be wire because this may hurt your pet's paws.

Fill the bottom of your chinchilla's cage with paper bedding. Don't use bedding made of pine or cedar wood chips. You should also give your pet places to rest and hide, such as a box or tube. Placing a quiet exercise wheel in the cage will help your chinchilla stay active.

Chinchillas can jump 6 feet (1.8 m) in the air!

Chinchillas like to climb. They love having different levels in their cage.

# What's for Lunch?

Pet chinchillas eat special food **pellets**. They also like to eat hay. You can find these foods at a pet store. Dried fruit, nuts, and seeds are good treats, but don't give them to your chinchilla too often. You may need to give your pet **vitamin C** drops in its water once a week. Vitamin C will help keep your pet healthy.

Chinchillas do something called coprophagy. This means they eat their own waste. They get more **nutrients** from their food this way.

## PET FOOD FOR THOUGHT

When chinchillas eat, they sit upright and hold their food in their front paws!

Using a hanging water bottle is an easy way to make sure your pet always has fresh water to drink. Just remember to refill it when it gets low!

# Happy and Healthy

Keeping your pet chinchilla happy and healthy is easy if you care for it properly. However, sometimes these little critters do get sick or hurt. If your chinchilla isn't eating or drinking, seems less active than usual, or is having trouble breathing, you should take your pet to the vet for a checkup.

A chinchilla's teeth never stop growing! Giving your pet safe toys to chew on, such as wood sticks, will keep its teeth from becoming too long.

PET FOOD FOR THOUGHT

Chinchillas may overheat if it's more than 75° Fahrenheit (24° Celsius) where they're kept. If your chinchilla gets too hot, you can cool it down in cool, not cold, water.

Chinchillas are social animals. Your pet will be happiest if it has another chinchilla to play with. If you get more than one chinchilla, it's best to get two males or two females.

17

# Keeping Clean

Chinchillas don't take baths like we do. They have a hard time drying off because their fur is so thick. Instead of using water to get clean, they use dust! Rolling around in dust helps them get rid of extra oil in their fur.

In the wild, chinchillas roll around in **volcanic** ash, but you can buy special chinchilla dust from a pet store. Put some dust into a large bowl twice a week and watch your chinchilla roll around and get clean.

PET FOOD FOR THOUGHT

Chinchillas are clean animals—they don't even have an odor! Change the bedding in your pet's cage at least once a week to keep it happy.

After your chinchilla takes a dust bath, remove the bowl from its cage to give it more room to run around.

# Playing with Your Pet

Pet chinchillas are quite active, and they do best in pairs. If you can only have one chinchilla, make sure you give it lots of attention and play with it often. Your pet will become very **attached** to you.

Chinchillas have long leg bones that break easily. Be very careful when holding your pet so you don't hurt it. Hold your chinchilla gently and never squash it. Keep your pet close to your body and always be calm.

**PET FOOD FOR THOUGHT**

Chinchillas love to play with toys. You can find many fun things for them to play with at a pet store.

It's a good idea to sit down when you hold your chinchilla. That way your pet will be close to the floor if it decides to jump out of your arms.

# Chinchilla Care Fact Sheet

- Always make sure your chinchilla has food and clean water to drink.

- Give your pet lots of safe toys to chew on.

- Chinchillas love to run around. Give your pet lots of time to play.

- Keep the area where your pet lives cool.

- Let your chinchilla take a dust bath twice a week to stay clean.

- Give your chinchilla lots of love and attention.

- Hold your pet carefully so you don't hurt it.

# Glossary

**allergic:** Having a bad bodily reaction to certain foods, animals, or surroundings.

**animal shelter:** A place where people take lost animals or animals without an owner.

**attached:** Closely joined in a social way.

**energy:** The power to work or act.

**extinction:** The state of no longer existing.

**flea:** A small, wingless bug that sucks the blood of the animal it lives on.

**nutrient:** Something taken in by a plant or animal that helps it grow and stay healthy.

**pellet:** A small piece of animal food.

**vitamin C:** A nutrient that helps the body fight illness and grow strong.

**volcanic:** Of or relating to a volcano, which is an opening in Earth's surface through which hot, liquid rock sometimes flows.

# Index

**A**
allergies, 6
Andes Mountains, 8

**B**
bedding, 12, 18

**C**
cage, 12, 13, 18, 19
coprophagy, 14

**D**
dust bath, 18, 19, 22

**E**
ears, 6, 7
exercise wheel, 12
extinction, 9

**F**
fleas, 7
food, 14, 22
fur, 4, 6, 7, 8, 9, 18

**H**
hay, 14
herds, 8

**K**
kit, 11

**P**
predator, 8

**S**
South America, 8, 9

**T**
tail, 6, 8
teeth, 16
toys, 16, 20, 22

**V**
vet, 16
vitamin C, 14

**W**
water, 14, 15, 16,
18, 22

Due to the changing nature of Internet links, PowerKids Press has developed an online list of websites related to the subject of this book. This site is updated regularly. Please use this link to access the list: www.powerkidslinks.com/owp/chin